Fabberoony Fizzy Pink

CHERRY WHYTOCK

PUFFIN

4 Tatiana

← a very
good fairy

With big
Kisses
xxx

PUFFIN BOOKS

Published by the Penguin Group
Penguin Books Ltd, 80 Strand, London WC2R 0RL, England
Penguin Group (USA) Inc., 375 Hudson Street, New York, New York 10014, USA
Penguin Group (Canada), 90 Eglinton Avenue East, Suite 700, Toronto, Ontario, Canada M4P 2Y3
(a division of Pearson Penguin Canada Inc.)
Penguin Ireland, 25 St Stephen's Green, Dublin 2, Ireland (a division of Penguin Books Ltd)
Penguin Group (Australia), 250 Camberwell Road, Camberwell, Victoria 3124, Australia
(a division of Pearson Australia Group Pty Ltd)
Penguin Books India Pvt Ltd, 11 Community Centre, Panchsheel Park,
New Delhi – 110 017, India
Penguin Group (NZ), cnr Airborne and Rosedale Roads, Albany, Auckland 1310, New Zealand
(a division of Pearson New Zealand Ltd)
Penguin Books (South Africa) (Pty) Ltd, 24 Sturdee Avenue, Rosebank, Johannesburg 2196,
South Africa

Penguin Books Ltd, Registered Offices: 80 Strand, London WC2R 0RL, England

www.penguin.com

First published 2006
1

Copyright © Cherry Whytock, 2006

Set in 14.5/ 20.5pt Adobe Leawood
Made and printed in England by Clays Ltd, St Ives plc

British Library Cataloguing in Publication Data
A CIP catalogue record for this book is available from the British Library

ISBN-13: 978-0-14131-902-5
ISBN-10: 0-141-31902-X

Contents

1

Hairy SCary Horrors

The most horrorvolting thing of all time has happened! Scary Mrs Cary (better known as Mrs SCary), my new form teacher at my new posh school, is back! She didn't explode after all! I was positive that was why she hadn't been into school for so long. Last time I saw her she was standing in front of the class all purple and trembly-wobbly and her steely rimmed glasses were flashing in the sunlight with her little icy eyes bulging behind them. It looked like she was going to go off BANG at any moment. I think that the reason Mrs SCary looked as if she was about to explode before she went on sick leave was on account of me explaining to her, very politely that:

a) My name is Fizzy Pink, not 'Felicity' as she kept calling me (well, actually my real name IS Felicity Pink but I mean, no one who's truly original like me would want to be called 'Felicity', would they?)

b) That I have made my uniform all sparkly and glamouroony to reflect my personality and

c) That my brain doesn't do maths.

And that was all it took to make her go so purple that she had to stay at home for ages. But now she's back again. GROTTYBAGS.

I look hard at her to see if she might have been stuck together again but I can't see any joins. She's explaining something really borifying about a number project she wants us to do so I have lots of time to think about other things. One of the things I think about is how I wish my best, best, bestest friend Pixie was here. We used to live almost next door to each other until my dad made pots of money decorating a stately home and we moved up in the world – which actually meant that we moved into a bigger house fifty miles away from Pixie

Sparklified uniform

and I had to come to this new posh school.

Pixie and I write each other loads of letters. When we are both fantabbymazingly famous our letters will definitely be made into a bestselling book.

I might write to Pixie now, just to pass the time. I think I'll tell her all the latest news about Cammy, a girl in my class who is deadly mean to me and tries to get everyone else to be mean to me too.

Everyone's scared of Cammy. Everyone except Daisy, that is. Daisy is the only person in this school who is halfway decent. She's really quiet and you might think that she would be shy but she isn't. When she smiles she's got big dimples, which are pretty fabberoony. Daisy sits next to me in class and together we stand up to Cammy.

Don't know why everyone else is

scared of Cammy. She's got this really stuck-up nose in the air and she talks about 'pehnies' instead of 'ponies' like proper people. She came to my birthday party on account of the Big Fat Fib Fairy making me make up a few little details about my family and our house . . . But in the end Cammy had a good time (except that she was sick – HA!) and she arrived at school the next morning with sequins stuck on her buttons, just like ME!

I thought she might be friendly for a bit after that but this morning she told the others that having freckles meant that your skin is 'blemished', whatever that might mean when it's at home. She was staring straight at me when she said it. But I don't care. She's probably just jealous because I've got loads of freckles. She'll be even more jealous in the summer when she sees how they get so big that they almost join

dearest darlingest Pixie

Cammy is still [flower]ing a [bee] (R / bee)

[pig] 2 me [hand]K and Mrs [scary face] SCARY

didn't go BANG after all—

She's come [arrows]← BACK ♪! [eye]

[fish] (fish / W) U were here. U [wood] wood

[he he face]←laugh at Mrs [scary face] scary. She is

[drawing]←poo(ey). [eye] am meant 2

[bee] doing $\frac{\frac{3}{2}+}{5\frac{1}{2}}$ ←sums now, better

stop. [pig] (new pen, at home now)—cammy says [freckled face]←freckles

R blemishes—she is so [food drawing] (/R)←food.

[eye] am making [worm] your

a tail warmer. ♡ [dots]

All my ♡ always—FIZZY x x x

Fizzy

together. I need to tell Pixie all about that. I bet Pixie will also be interested to hear that Mrs SCary didn't blow up after all.

I can hear a grumpy old voice saying 'FELICITY' and I think, Ooops-a-bloomin'-daisy, that must be Mrs SCary and she must mean me, so I look up and smile my most glamouroony smile and begin to say, 'Do you mean me, Mrs SCary? Because if you do, my name is Fizz–'

Pixie

7

Mrs SCary helping with maths

But Mrs SCary doesn't let me finish. Instead she shouts, 'Would you PLEASE get on with your number project, if it's not TOO much trouble.' I look closely at her to see if she's changing colour at all. So far she is pretty much just pink.

'Well, you see,' I say, 'the thing is that I'm sort of allergic to numbers – they make me hyperventilate . . .' I'm not actually completely sure what 'hyperventilate' means but it's just such a fabberoony word and I can feel that by using it I've got everyone's attention.

'. . . And hyperventilating will probably make me take off and float around the room, which, as I'm sure you will understand, could be very dangerous on account of bashing into things and hurting myself . . .'

The room's gone deadly quiet and Mrs SCary is getting pinker by the second. She's sort of opening and closing her mouth a lot like Pixie's pet snake does when it's pretending to bite you. She looks as if she's hoping some words might come out but they seem to have got stuck somewhere. Then she coughs an enormous cough and, with her teeth sort of clenched, she says, 'You WILL do this project, FELICITY, even if I have to come and hold on to your feet to stop you "floating around" as you put it. Do you understand?'

There's a horrible wheezy giggle from the back of the room and I know it's coming from Cammy. Some of the boys are giggling too. But boys don't count.

The thing is that I don't really like the idea of trying to do maths with Mrs SCary hanging on to my feet and last time I answered back was the time that she went purple and wobbly AND she gave me a detention. So I smooth down my school skirt that I personally sparklified with diamanté and glittery rhinestones, flick my curly red hair over my shoulder, look Mrs SCary straight in her icy cold eyes and say, 'OK.' (Which is Mrs SCary's least favourite word – ooops!)

2
Dad Wiggles and Mum Giggles

When I get home from school there's a letter from Pixie waiting for me. She says she's saving up for a big Christmas present for me, which is dead exciting. I'm making her a sparkly belt with flowers on.

While I'm reading my letter my mum starts making toast soldiers for the Splat's tea. The Splat is my brother. He is two and

The Splat splattering egg

even though he's a boy he is quite cool. His real name is Jack but I call him the Splat because he's always splattering stuff, like his food or Dad's paint.

Don't want to do any boring old homework after reading Pixie's letter so I go to see what my dad's doing. I can hear him singing one of his Elvis songs which probably means he's painting something somewhere. He paints a lot on account of him being a decorator.

'What's up, Fizzy Freckles?' he asks when I find him. He's in the Splat's room. He's painting everything yellow, even the ceiling. When it's dry he says I can help him paint on huge blue fish to make it look like the seaside. 'You've got a face as long as one of Mrs Fossil's stockings,' he says. This makes me laugh. Mrs Fossil lives next door and she always has really wrinkly brown woolly stockings on so they probably are fantabbymazingly long.

'Nothing much,' I say. 'Except that I got all my maths wrong because there was an evil witch in the classroom and she cast this spell on me and the spell made me add up all the things I was meant to take away and then the witch flew all round the room and . . .'

My dad has stopped singing and his eyebrows have gone all serious.

'Fizzy,' he says, 'you know what your mum and I think about telling fibs . . . there wasn't a witch in the classroom now was there?'

'Well . . .' I say because Mrs SCary is almost a witch, but I don't think she's got a broomstick. At least if she has got a broomstick she must leave it in the bike shed before she comes in to class.

'No . . .' I say, 'I s'pose there wasn't . . . But it *felt* like there was because something made my maths go all wrong . . .' I'm feeling a bit grottybags now because Mum and Dad are always telling me that Fibs Are Bad. But, honestly, sometimes these Big Fat Fibs just pop out of nowhere. I mean, all I do is open my mouth and the Fib Fairy gets these fibs to gallop across the country-side and land up in my mouth.

I say, 'Sorry, Dad,' and I sit down on the floor with Petal.

Petal's our bulldog. He can look dead scary but he isn't really. I'm making him some stretchy sequinned leg warmers as

Petal in legwarmers

a Christmas present. Hope he'll like them. Dad climbs down the stepladder. He's got his paint- brush in his hand and he's holding it like a microphone. He comes up to Petal and me and starts singing 'You Ain't Nothin' but a Hound Dog' to Petal. It's one of his Elvis songs and he makes these fabberoony moves while he's singing. His knees go all bendy and he sticks his bottom out and sort of wiggles it about. Then he makes his feet go all jumpy and he does something weird with his shoulders.

'Come on, Fizzy,' he says, 'there's nothing like a spot of old Elvis to brighten up the day – come on, come and stamp those daisy roots!'

15

Dad often says funny rhyming things. 'Daisy roots' means 'boots'. He pulls me up and we start jumping about singing 'Hound Dog' as loud as we can.

'That's it,' says Dad. 'Now shake your shoulders like this . . . and then step back and wiggle a bit – like this . . .' We're jumping about and wiggling like anything. Dad's showing me how to do the backwards steps when I look up and see Mum at the door. I grab hold of Dad's arm just as he's about to swing round and make another move. I stop. He stops.

'Oh, my Elvis!' sighs Mum from the doorway. 'I could hear that old "Hound Dog" right down in the kitchen . . . Jack came over all excited and splattered his egg across the floor so we thought we'd come up and join the party.'

'Come and give old Baz a smackeroony,' says Dad. My mum comes over and gives

Dad a great big sloppy kiss and I try not to look. The Splat's too young to notice. I think it's dead embarrassifying.

'You're a Princess, Reenie, and no mistake,' says Dad and he gives her a little squeeze. My mum is quite squeezy because of being sort of roundish. If I'm feeling a bit scared about something – which is hardly ever because I, Fizzy Pink, am the bravest person you are ever likely

squeezy Mum with sweeties in her pocket

to meet – but, IF I'm feeling scared then my mum's lap is the best place to be in the entire universe because she's like a big squishy sofa. And she always smells sort of yummy. And she's often got sweeties in her pocket.

'Come and have your tea,' says Mum when she and Dad have stopped slobber-ifying, 'and then you can tell us all about your day, Fizzy. How are all those nice little girls who came to your party getting on?'

'Who?' I ask as we go downstairs.

'Now, what were their names? Oh, yes, there was that poor little thing who was poorly. Cammy, wasn't that her name? How was she today?'

'She said freckles are blemishes,' I say.

'Oh, dear,' says Mum, 'that wasn't very nice, was it? Especially when we all know that freckles are little splashes of magic

18

paint from fairies' paintbrushes, don't we?'
I don't answer because I'm not sure that
she's right about that one. 'Anyway,' she
goes on, 'there was that little sweetness
called Daisy, wasn't there? Now *she* was
ever such a quiet, nice little thing. *She*
must be a special friend, isn't she?'

'Sort of,' I say. And when I think about
it, I kind of have to admit that if it wasn't
for Daisy, school would be the MOST
horrorvolting place on the planet. She's
really nice, Daisy – but I'm not sure that I
should tell Pixie that.

3
Homework Hullaballoo

I'm a bit late into school this morning because the Splat had a tantrum at breakfast. He tipped his bowl of porridge on to Petal's head and it all got stuck in the emerald-studded ear-flaps I made him. It took hours to get Petal cleaned up. When I get to the classroom Mrs SCary is already there.

'FELICITY,' she says with that 'Don't-you-dare-to-tell-me-your-name-is-Fizzy' look in her eyes, 'you're late!'

'I'm sorry, Mrs SCary,' I say and I squeeze my mouth tight shut so that the Big Fat Fib Fairy can't get in there and make me tell a big fib about why I'm not on time.

'Is that *all* you've got to say for yourself?' says Mrs SCary, glaring at me. If I wasn't as brave as a lion this might make me a bit wobbly, but I look at Daisy and she gives me a little dimply smile, which makes me feel much better. I take a deep breath.

'Our bulldog got porridge in his emerald-studded ear-flaps and it took ages to get them clean,' I begin.

'Don't be ridiculous!' squawks Mrs SCary. 'If you're going to make up a story you might at least have the presence of mind to make it something believable!'

'But it's true!' I gasp. I mean, honestly, here I am being completely brillybags and not letting the Big Fat Fib Fairy make me tell a fib and Mrs SCary doesn't believe me anyway!

I see that Daisy has put up her hand. 'Excuse me, Mrs SCary,' she says, 'but Fizzy does have a bulldog with sparkly emerald ear-flaps. He's called Petal . . .'

One or two of the other girls in my class are murmuring, 'Mmmm, she has, it is true . . .'

Big Fat Fib Fairy

22

Mrs SCary is going a bit pink now but she's still glaring at me. I look at Daisy and try to give her a little secret smile, to say 'thank you'.

'I made his ear-flaps myself,' I say bravely and Mrs SCary gets pinker and pinker and I think there might be steam coming out of her ears.

'Class – I don't want to hear any more of this . . .' she says, pulling at the neck of her jumper as if she's trying to get more air. 'This morning we are going to do something NEW!' Now she's polishing her glasses on account of them being a bit steamed up. 'We're going to have Sharing Time!'

I'm thinking, What might Sharing Time be when it's at home? If it means letting grottybags old Cammy borrow my starryfied and glitteryfied fantabby trainers – then excuse me, but I don't think I'll be taking

sparklified trainers

part. I'm just about to explain this to Mrs SCary when she puts her glasses back on, glares at me and sort of barks, 'SIT DOWN NOW, FELICITY!' So I do.

'What I mean by "Sharing Time" is that each week we are all going to sit round in a circle and one by one we will tell each other something of interest that has happened to us . . .'

I put my hand up straight away because this could be my big chance to tell everyone about all the fabberoony stuff I have done. They'll all realize that I'm not the dim witty that Cammy makes me out to be but that I, Fizzy Amber Jade Pink, am a truly *fascinating* person. But Mrs SCary doesn't seem to want to see me. Instead she tells us to all 'gather round and sit in a circle'.

Everybody goes and sits down really fast. By the time I get there the circle is so tightly packed that there isn't any room for me. Cammy gives me one of her silly stuck-up-nose-in-the-air smug smiles. I'll show her. I climb over everyone into the middle of the circle and sit down.

'FELICITY . . . !' roars Mrs SCary.

Before she can frizzle me up with the flames that are coming out of her hairy nostrils, Daisy grabs hold of my sparkly skirt and pulls me into a little space next to her.

And then we begin.

4
My Magical Granny

Something spookifying is happening. Either Mrs SCary has gone completely blind on one side or I have become invisible. I've put my hand up at least a zillion times during Sharing Time and I still haven't been asked to say a single sausage!

Everybody else in my whole class is pretending to find Cammy (who has been talking for AGES) interesting. Can't think why. She's going on and on about how wonderful she is at riding and how she's won 'billions of rosettes'. She brags about the judge at the 'pehnie show' who told her she had 'a wonderful seat', which sounds really rude to me. Now she's telling us how she taught her pony to take a bow and how the crowds all cheered when he did it. Show-off.

I'm looking really closely at my sparklified skirt to see if I could fit any more diamanté in between the pleats because this is way more interesting than listening to Cammy piffling on about her 'pehnie's fetlocks', whatever they might be. Then I hear, 'FELICITY!'

I only look up because Mrs SCary has said 'FELICITY' so loudly, not because it's my name, because it isn't. But then I realize that it's MY turn!

I jump straight up and sort of bounce into the centre of the circle. Everyone else stayed where they were to do their bit but this is my big chance and I want to be sure that everyone can see me properly. I notice that the sun is making the sequins on my buttons sparkle nicely. I twirl about for a moment and then I begin. I'm going to tell the class about the glamouroony dresses that my mum makes and how I help her sometimes. But then somehow that doesn't seem exciting enough and my mouth starts saying, 'Once upon a time . . .'

'You're not supposed to be telling a made-up story,' says Cammy in her nasty, sneering voice.

'It's not a made-up story,' I say, sounding brave but feeling a bit wibbly-wobbly because I'm pretty certain that the Big Fat Fib Fairy is about to pop into my mouth.

'It's about what happened to me but it happened once upon a time.'

Mrs SCary sighs and then she says, 'Carry on, FELICITY.'

'. . . There was a huge crumbling castle . . .'

'Where was that, then?' says Cammy. 'Next door to your little house, I suppose!' And some of the others start giggling.

Fizzy at Sharing Time flashing her 'diamonds'

Mrs SCary actually glares at Cammy and the others and they shut up. This makes me feel sort of important – everyone is looking at me now and listening properly. I can't tell them any old boring everyday sort of story. So, here I go . . .

'And in this castle lived an old, old woman with grizzly hair and skin as wrinkly as a mouldy apple. The walls of her castle were covered in fabulous jewels . . .'

'Yeah, right!' says Cammy, but under her breath this time.

'. . . and they glittered and sparkled all day and all night. Now this old, old woman had special powers and she could make fantastic things happen if she wanted to. She could turn poodles into ponies –' I can see Cammy is looking a bit more interested now – 'and worms into poisonous snakes . . . and pebbles into

sweeties. One day she
decided to store
some of her magic
powers in one of the
diamonds that were
all around her on
the walls of her
castle so that
whoever owned
that diamond would
have those magic
powers. Not long after that, the old, old
woman vanished.'

MrsScary breathing
very loud

I look all round the circle and everyone is
gazing at me with their mouths wide open.
Except for Mrs SCary, that is. She's got her
hand over her eyes and she's breathing
very loudly. I can tell she's not asleep
though. I think she might be spellbound by
my fabberoony story and that she is just
longing to hear what happens next.

31

I go on. 'Now that old, old woman was my grandmother and she disappeared in a puff of smoke the day I was born. Before she went she told everyone that she wanted me to have that very magical diamond. That is why, to this day, I wear diamonds and sparklified bits on my clothes because one of these diamonds –' I point to my skirt and twirl round so that everyone can see – 'is THE diamond with all its magic powers that my granny gave me . . .'

'So which one of the "diamonds" on your skirt is the magic one then?' asks Cammy in her stuck-up voice and some of the other girls, who were nice to me at my birthday party but are still really scared of Cammy, giggle at me.

'It's a secret!' I say. 'And my granny told me never to tell anyone . . .'

'I thought your granny had disappeared

in a puff of smoke!' says Cammy, and I'm beginning to think, Uh-oh, that Big Fat Fib Fairy has really landed me in it this time . . . and I don't think my granny would be very happy to hear that she had gone up in a puff of smoke, especially not when she actually lives in Basingstoke . . . oh, CRUMPETS! What am I going to do next . . .?

about to be killed stone cold dead

Well, Mrs SCary comes to my rescue, sort of. She suddenly claps her hands and says, 'Now, children, that's quite enough of all that! I want you all to go back to your desks and FELICITY will come up to the front of the class please.'

This is it, I think as I trudge up to

Mrs SCary's desk. She's probably going to put me in detention for ever and ever and make me write six zillion lines for telling fibs. Then she will tell me that I am never to come to school again wearing my glitteryfied uniform . . . I am so busy imagining all the dreadful things that she is going to do to me on account of the Big Fat Fib that I don't think I've heard properly when Mrs SCary says, '. . . So I want you to take the class guinea pig home with you this evening and look after him, for the next ten days, on your own. I hope, FELICITY, that this will give you a sense of duty and responsibility and maybe this will be the beginning of a new phase in which you will always be sensible and tell the truth!'

'Gosh!' says Daisy when I sit back down again. 'Doesn't Mrs SCary think your story was true?'

dearest darlingest Pixie

Guess wot???? We 🐟 [haddock] sharing

🕐 [1] time! 👁 [I] shared about 💎s [diamonds].
👁 [I] told a lot of fibs. T🐔 [hen] 🛏 [bed] t🎩 [hat]

😠 [Mrs Scary] ← Mrs Scary

👁👁 [eyes] could 👁👁 ←look after the

🦔 ←guinea pig Goliath
(can't draw him, sorry) 4 a ⚫ ←hole

ten days!! 👁 [I] bet your 🐍 [snake] 🪵 [tail warmer]

like 2 🪖 meat Goliath. Do U
think your 🐍 [snake] 🪵 [tail warmer] eat 🦔 [hedgehog]?

Hope 🪢 [knot]!! We 🐟 [haddock] LIVER
4 lunch - double double YUCK.
👁 [I] will ♡ U 4ever - Fizzy

                    x   x

'Um . . .' I say, 'maybe not. I don't think she's very clever.' I whisper this last bit in case Mrs SCary can hear. Daisy giggles and her dimples go all dimply.

'Would your granny mind if you showed me the magic diamond one day?' she asks.

I say, 'No, I'm sure she wouldn't!' but I feel a bit grottybags. Pixie would be furious with me for telling such a Great Big Fat Fib.

5
Guinea Pig a Go-Go

'Oh, isn't he absolutely cutesy-wutesy?' says my mum. 'Dear little thing!' She's looking at Goliath, the class guinea pig. He's in his cage and I've brought him up to Mum's sewing room. He's sort of grey and white and fluffy in places. He's got sparkly black eyes just like two beads.

'You must have been ever such a good girl to be chosen to look after him, Fizzy.'

'Er . . . ye-es,' I say because I still don't really understand why Mrs SCary thinks Goliath will help my sense of responsibility. And there's no way he's big enough to chase away the Big Fat Fib Fairy! (Anyway, Daisy told me later she thought my bit of Sharing was the best. I showed her how to do a few of Dad's moves as a kind of 'thank you'.)

'Now, we'll keep Goliath in the back porch,' says Mum. 'He'll be everso snug there and he won't get into a muddle with all these costumes.'

The reason our house is full of costumes is on account of my mum's sister, Auntie Bev. Auntie Bev is not a bit like my mum. Auntie Bev is all thin and jingly. She wears mad, weird, patchwork clothes and you always know when she's around because all her bangles and necklaces clank about when she moves. She does acty things all over the place (a bit like Dad pretending to be Elvis, but not half as much fun) and she says that she is an 'actaw'. My mum doesn't do acty things, she makes clothes – she's a dressmaker and she's making all the costumes for Auntie Bev's Christmas show.

I love it when Mum's making clothes. There are always all sorts of exciting bits

Aunty Bev being acty

and pieces left over. Mum lets me use anything she puts in her shiny red Odds and Bods box and I can already see that there are loads of leftover sequins and crystal beads and bits of glittery ribbon. I can't wait to start sewing something with all this glamouroony, fantabby stuff! Perhaps I'll make Goliath a sparkly sequinned coat . . .

'Take Goliath down now, there's a good girl, and let me get on with this outfit,' says Mum.

So I carry the cage down to the porch and find this cosy little spot on the shelf where we keep all our wellie boots. My boots are pink so I think that Goliath would like to sit next to them best. When I've put the cage down I think he looks a bit sort of sad. So I go and find a piece of purple shiny material from Mum's Odds and Bods box and put that over his cage to cheer him up until I have time to make his glamouroony coat. But he still looks sad. I wonder if he feels like one of those people who were slaves in the olden days on account of him being all sort of 'imprisoned'. I remember Mrs SCary telling us in our history

Goliath looking sad.

40

lesson that the slaves were 'liberated', which means set free. So I lean down and ask Goliath if he would like to be liberated too. He makes a little squeak when I ask him so I know that means 'Yes'. I'm certain Mrs SCary would be really pleased that I've remembered this bit of her history lesson.

'What I'll do then, Goliath,' I tell him, 'is just to leave the door of your cage a teeny-weeny bit open in case you suddenly want to be liberated in the night. Then you can sniffle around in the garden whenever you feel like it and come back to your cage when you get tired.' He looks miles happier when I've done that so I give him some food and go and visit Mrs Fossil next door.

I don't have to knock at Mrs Fossil's door any more because she says I can come round any time. Besides, she's a bit 'mutton jeff' as my dad says, which means deaf, so there's not much point knocking anyway.

Petal has come with me. He likes Mrs Fossil's house on account of all the stuffed weasels she keeps in her front hall. He likes growling at them and pretending they're real.

'Hellooooo!' I shout. 'Helloooo!'

'Well, if it isn't my old friend Frizzy!' says Mrs Fossil. She's watching dog racing on the telly. I don't bother telling her that my name is 'Fizzy' because she never gets it right. 'So what's been happening at that school of yours then, eh?'

Mrs Fossil watching dog racing on the telly

'We had Sharing Time,' I say.

'OOO!' says Mrs Fossil. 'That sounds exotic!'

'Does it?' I ask.

'Oh, yes! Lime is way more exotic than lemon. If you had come in and said you'd been sharing a lemon I wouldn't have been very interested but sharing a lime now . . .'

'N-n-no,' I say. 'Not lime – time. It meant we had to talk about something in front of the rest of the class.'

'What, while you were sucking on the lime?' asks Mrs Fossil.

'Um . . .' I say and I think I'd better change the subject. This is all getting too complicated.

'Shall I make you a cup of tea, Mrs Fossil?' I ask and, amazingly, this time she hears exactly what I've said.

6

My Weird Weekend

Yesterday two things happened.

1) WAS A GOOD THING: Auntie Bev is going to make me The Star of her show – fabberoony!

2) WAS A BAD THING: Goliath has gone missing – gulp.

Today is Saturday.

Things that happen next:

1) I jump about a bit (because of being excited about being The Star).

2) I search in all the wellies for Goliath – don't find him.

3) I jump about a bit more with big grin on my face (because of The Star thing).

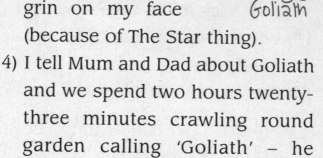

searching for Goliath

4) I tell Mum and Dad about Goliath and we spend two hours twenty-three minutes crawling round garden calling 'Goliath' – he doesn't answer.

5) I look in all kitchen cupboards and under table and chairs for Goliath – don't find him.

6) I practise singing starry sorts of songs.

7) Mum suggests that I put small pile of guinea pig food in a cosy-looking box and wait for Goliath to come and eat it – he doesn't, but Petal does.

8) I give Auntie Bev a great big smackeroony when she arrives on account of starring in her show.

9) I make double sure that Goliath isn't back in his cage – he isn't.

10) I do a song and dance routine for Auntie Bev.

11) She tells me that being-a-star-in-her-show-means-that-I-have-to-stand-completely-still-at-the-back-of-the-stage-without-saying-anything-and-with-my-arms-and-legs-out-straight-pretending-to-be-a-little-twinkly-star-in-the-night-sky.

12) I have tantrum.

dearest darlingest Pixie

[well] +Well!! 2 REEEEALLY [pooey]

things have happened — 1st [eye] was

going 2 [bee] THE/2 [star] in Aunty Bev's

[tree] ←Christmas show. NOW [eye] am KNOT!!

T[hen] [eye] had an [bulb] ←idea, [needle] ←sew

[eye] LIBERATED Goliath [hand] now

he has [cloud] ←vanished. Mrs [face]

will kill me stone cold dead.

[dagger] ←dagger
←me
←blood

What [shell/2] [eye] do ??? [shell/2] [eye] [dress] ←dress

up [hand] pretend 2 [bee] the [burst/2]? Also

[eye] [log] like 2 [bee] a [star] and [knot] ←KNOT

stone cold dead — POO. HELP!

♡ u loads — Fizzy x This could be my

last letter x ever — goodbye....

13) I get sent to my room.
14) I wake up on Sunday morning knowing that I am not going to become fantabbymazingly famous after all. POO.
15) I spend all day searching for and worrying about one lost guinea pig. I don't find him. Mum doesn't find him. Dad doesn't find him. Tomorrow Mrs SCary will kill me Stone Cold Dead because I've liberated Goliath. DOUBLE POO.

7

Fear, Fleas and French Toast

The thing about Monday morning is that when you know you are going to be killed Stone Cold Dead it's best to stay in bed. But Mum won't let me.

'I don't want any nonsense now, Fizzy,' she says when she pulls back my glittery satin bedspread. 'You've just got to be all grown up and tell Mrs Cary exactly what's happened to poor Goliath.' I'm not so sure now that Mrs SCary will be pleased about me remembering her history lesson when the slaves were liberated. Then Mum sighs, which doesn't make me feel any better. 'I'm sure she won't be *that* cross,' she says, 'and you mustn't worry – Goliath has probably gone to some happy guinea pig playground in the sky . . . You can tell Mrs Cary that your dad and I will be happy to buy a new pet for the class. So, there you are! Now hurry up and get dressed . . . there's a letter waiting for you downstairs.'

Goliath in heaven

This sounds quite interesting but I say 'herumph' as I get up. Just to make my point. I put on my uniform – even my

50

glamouroony diamanté-trimmed skirt and my shirt with the sparkly buttons don't make me feel any better. How can I tell Mrs SCary that I haven't been 'responsible' or 'dutiful' about looking after Goliath? How can I explain to her that I thought it would be a good idea to liberate him instead?

'Hurry down for your breakfast, Fizzy,' Mum calls up the stairs.

'Don't want any beastly breakfast,' I mumble as I stamp down to the kitchen.

I go to check Goliath's cage, just in case he's come back in the night. He hasn't. Then I pick my letter up off the hall table. It's from Pixie. She says she's sorry to hear that Mrs SCary was back but she didn't think people often went purple and exploded on their own.

Dad's already in the kitchen. He's singing 'Jailhouse Rock', which seems like a good choice. Mrs SCary'll probably put me in prison later today before she kills me Stone Cold Dead. She'll find me guilty of Gross Negligence to Guinea Pigs. I'll have nothing but bread and water for the rest of my short life . . .

Mum has made French toast and it smells yummy. I suppose it might be a

making moves with Baz

good idea to eat lots now on account of probably not having anything decent to eat ever again. I have five slices.

'Goodness gracious!' says my mum. 'You must have hollow legs! Now, come on or you'll be late for school again and Mrs Cary will be cross.'

Not half as cross as she'll be when she hears about Goliath, I'm thinking.

Just before we go, Dad starts doing his 'Hound Dog' moves and he makes me join in.

'That's it, Fizzy,' he says, 'you could be Elvis's little sister making moves like that!'

'Come ON, Fizzy,' yells Mum. 'Hurry up, do!' So I pick up my bag and take what could be my final walk to our pink van.

Actually, it's made me feel a little bit better doing the Elvis moves. I sit in the van with the Splat strapped in the back and Petal sitting on my feet. I think how

sad it is that I may not live long enough
to make any Elvis moves ever again . . .

I'm not late at school after all. I'm quite
early. Everyone is still in the playground.
I see Daisy and give her a little wave. She
waves back and I go over and ask her if
she would like to practise some Elvis
moves with me as this will definitely be
my Last Chance to Dance.

'Oh, Fizzy, I'd love to!' she says and she
does that big smile that makes her
dimples go all dimply. We start wiggling
and jiggling all round the playground.

'How sad!' I hear a voice say. 'Are
you two ill or something? The way
you're jumping around it looks like
you've got fleas or bugs or both – look,
everybody . . .' Of course, the horrible
nose-in-the-air voice is coming from
Cammy. She goes on, '. . . look, everyone

– Fizzy and Daisy have got fleas! Look at them jumping about trying to get rid of them! Hope you haven't given them to that cute little guinea pig! What's the matter with you, Fizzy? Are the bugs biting?' HA HA HA.

Now I, Fizzy Pink, am as brave as a superhero but why did Cammy have to mention Goliath and make me feel all wibbly-wobbly again? And why does she

Fizzy and Daisy making Elvis moves

always have to be so mean and nasty just when Daisy and I are having fun? But if I am about to be killed Stone Cold Dead I suppose it doesn't really matter anyway. So Daisy and I carry on making our Elvis moves and I notice that some of the others are trying to wiggle and jiggle just like us. Cammy is looking furious. I'm trying to think of something dead mean and squashing to say to her when the bell for registration goes and we all have to hurry to our classroom.

'CLASS . . .' squawks Mrs SCary, 'will you all gather round now for this week's Sharing Time. Now that you all understand what you are meant to be doing, I hope that we will have a more *sensible* session –' she's glaring at me as she says this – 'than we did last week.'

I trudge off towards the Sharing Circle. I bet Mrs SCary will choose me straight away this time and she'll want me to talk about Goliath. I better get ready to be killed Stone Cold Dead . . . I think I might be going to be sick . . .

But then Daisy smiles at me and I hurry to sit next to her. She gets chosen to Share first. She gives me a big grin and then she tells the rest of the class about learning to do Elvis moves with ME!

Almost everyone (except Cammy) looks really interested. One of the boys asks Daisy to do an Elvis wiggle and she does! Everyone (except Cammy and some of her soppy friends) claps when she has finished. Then Daisy gives me another big grin when she sits down. I stop feeling quite so wobbly but only for a little bit because suddenly Mrs SCary decides that it's my turn to Share something.

8

Starring the Big Fat Fib Fairy

After Daisy has finished Sharing her moves with the class Mrs SCary decides that it's my turn to Share something. She clears her throat and says, 'Now, FELICITY, I feel sure that you would like to tell the rest of the class about your new responsible role?' There's a nasty glint in her mean, snake-like eyes. Any minute now she will be killing me Stone

Cold Dead . . . unless . . . I know she wants me to talk about Goliath but she hasn't actually mentioned his name, has she? She said something about a 'responsible role' and being The Star in Auntie Bev's show is a responsible role, isn't it?

the BFF fairy whispering in Fizzy's ear

I stand up . . . 'My Auntie Bev is an actor.' I look round the group and everyone looks properly impressed. Mrs

SCary looks a bit confused as Auntie Bev is definitely not a guinea pig. 'She's brilliant but you may not have heard of her on account of "Auntie Bev" not being her stage name . . . Anyway . . . my Auntie Bev is putting on a Christmas show and I am going to be The Star! Yes, that's right . . .' I say when I see Mrs SCary's eyebrows shoot up, 'I am The Star of her Christmas show. I shall be doing a very important starring song and a dance routine.' I do a little Elvis-type wiggle and *somebody* laughs. 'I am having a spectacular costume made for me – something that is fit for a Very Important Star with loads of glitter and shiny bits – and I may even have a backing group . . .' I look across at Mrs SCary who hasn't moved a muscle while I've been Sharing. 'Unfortunately I may be unable to do all my homework on account of having to go to so many

rehearsals and becoming overtired . . .'
I'm quite pleased with this bit. Mrs SCary
doesn't look very pleased though.
'Because, of course, being a superstar can
be a very tiring business . . .'

'So when is this show that you're being
a *superstar* in?' asks Cammy. It's not very
nice the way she says *'superstar'*. I tell
her the date anyway because she doesn't
scare me, does she? No, she does not! I'm
just about to tell everyone *where* Auntie
Bev's Christmas show is being shown
when I suddenly think, UH-OH!

I stand there with my mouth wide open
while this spookifying thought stamps
about in my head: all that stuff about
being a proper star was a GREAT BIG FAT
FIB! I sit down really hard in the hopes of
squashing the Big Fat Fib but it's no use.
There it is! A Huge Fib! All Big and Black
and Horrorvolting! I'm not THE Star, am

I? I'm *a* star, which is something quite different. Why does the Big Fat Fib Fairy keep doing this to me? She goes on popping these whopping great fibs into my mouth without even asking me first!

'Thank you, FELICITY,' says Mrs SCary. 'I was going to tell you to sit down but I see that you already have . . . I must say that wasn't the Responsible Subject that I meant you to share with the class but now I see that we haven't enough time to hear about Goliath . . . I'm sure your show will be a great success.'

There's something about the way she says 'great success' with that hissing 'ssssss' that makes it sound like she doesn't mean it one little bit.

Daisy with her glitter pen

All through the rest of the day I keep thinking about my Big Fat Fibs. I think about telling Daisy what I've done but I decide not to at the last minute. She's not my best, bestest friend because Pixie is and Pixie isn't here. Daisy is really nice though and she lets me try her new glitter pen at lunchtime, which makes me feel better.

Our last lesson is history and Mrs SCary talks some more about the Slave Trade. Then she talks about 'liberating the slaves' and I get that sinking feeling in my tummy again. What if I never find Goliath? How was I supposed to know that if I liberated him he would disappear? Then I get all collywobbly worrying about whether he's got anything to eat. Poor Goliath! He might be cold and starving. I wish I *had* made him a glittery coat – at least I would know that he was warm. He might be stuck somewhere. I heard of someone whose guinea pig got stuck down a rabbit hole for a WEEK before they found him. He was all skinny when they pulled him out . . . I look across at Daisy. I wonder if she would understand that I was trying to be kind to Goliath but that it all went wrong?

She smiles her dimply smile back at me, but I'm still not sure that I should tell her.

Suddenly the bell goes and it's the end of school. I start packing my things up. I was feeling grottybags when I came in this morning on account of probably being killed Stone Cold Dead. Now I'm feeling even more grottybags on account of the Fib Fairy and what she made me say about being The Star. I really want to go home and write to Pixie. I wish I could phone her but we're not allowed to

Cammy

phone each other because Dad says we talk too much. I wonder what Pixie would say about the Big Fat Fibs?

I'm just closing my locker when Cammy comes barging up to me and says, 'I hope you're looking after that dear little guinea pig properly because I'M looking after him next, you know!'

OH, GOODY GOODY GUMDROPS.

9
Slithery Star Suit

After checking to see if Goliath is back in his cage, which he isn't, the only thing I want to do when I get home is to write to Pixie. But I can't. As soon as Mum and I walk in through the door, Auntie Bev arrives.

'Daaaarlings!' she squawks. She pushes the back door as wide as it will go and she stands in the doorway with her arms stretched out. Her bracelets are clanking around and she looks like she's wearing somebody's bedcover.

I think she's hoping that I will run up to her and be hugged. Don't want to. I know it's not her fault that I liberated Goliath and told a huge Big Fat Fib, but it feels like it is. If she hadn't asked me to be a soppy star in her soppy Christmas show the Big Fat Fib Fairy would never have made me say all that stuff about being The Star. Honestly.

Aunty Bev jingle jangling

'You just cannot BELIEVE the day I've had!' she says.

Bet it wasn't as grottybags as mine, I'm thinking, but I don't say anything.

She sweeps into the room and whooshes her bedcover, or whatever it is, over her shoulder. There's this jingle-jangle noise from her bracelets when she puts her hands up to tidy her hair. Dad says it looks like 'there's a bird in her barnet', which means that her hair's a bit wild and fuzzy. Also, she's got some feathers stuck in it today.

Then she starts. 'My life is in TATTERS! The CAST will never be ready in time. They haven't learned their lines . . . They don't come to rehearsals when they should . . . Oooooh, I just don't know HOW I'm going to cope . . . ' She stops squawking and stands dead still in the middle of the kitchen. One of her hands is over her eyes, the other is over where her heart is. She's swaying a bit. If we didn't know her really well Mum and I might be a bit worrified now, but instead Mum says, 'Come and sit down and I'll make you a nice cup of tea. Then you can have a look at some of the costumes . . .'

'Daaaarling!' she groans at my mum. 'If it wasn't for you, I don't know WHAT I would do . . . you're the only one who UNDERSTANDS . . .' and she flops down on to one of our kitchen chairs. Her earrings swing about for quite a long time after she's sat down.

Mum makes some tea and Auntie Bev looks a bit brighter. 'And how is my favourite little niece then?' she asks. 'Is she a happy little bunnikins, or is she a miserable little munchkin?' She makes her mouth go right down at the corners when she says this. She looks quite funny. She almost makes me smile. 'Has Mummy made your lovely star outfit then?' A new sparkly outfit?! I look at Mum. Mum looks dead proud.

'I've just got the last little bits to do and then it will be ready!' she says. 'You're going to love it, Fizzy Freckles – it's everso shiny! Why don't you run up and fetch it now? Then we can have a good old try on and Auntie Bev can see how beautiful you look!'

This sounds more interesting.

I run upstairs and start searching in Mum's sewing room. I'm half hoping that Goliath might have hopped upstairs and that I'll find him hiding in Mum's sewing basket. He isn't and I don't. Now then . . . where is this glamouroony-sounding outfit? 'I can't find it!' I shout down the stairs.

Space baby suit

70

Mum shouts back, 'It's the one on the back of my sewing chair . . . you must be able to see it!'

OH!

I go over to her chair and pick up this droopy silver thing. Is this it? Is this my fabulous star costume? It's only a kind of all-in-one bodysuit with arms and legs attached and it's just plain old boring silver! I put it on and look in the mirror. UGH! I look sort of slimy like Pixie's pet snake (except that Pixie's snake looks way nicer). The material's all slithery and yuckyvolting. This costume looks like one of those all-in-one baby suits – I look like a BABY from outer space! A SPACE BABY . . . I look like a space baby and I DON'T WANT TO! I want to look fridgey cool and fabberoony, not all babified and silly.

I slither downstairs.

'Oh, my WORD!' says Auntie Bev when she sees me. 'Look at this SPECTACULAR star!' She wraps her arms around herself and gives herself a squeeze.

Mum's looking all happy and smiley. I'm feeling grottybags.

'Now, hold your arms out like this . . .' says Auntie Bev. She stands up and makes her arms and legs into a sort of star shape. She looks silly. I do what she says. I feel silly too. 'Magnificent!' she says. 'Reenie daaaarling, you've made my day! With all your beautiful costumes I JUST KNOW that my little show is going to be a HUGE SUCCESS!'

Well, I think, she's changed her tune and all because she's seen me looking like a space baby! I don't want to say anything though, because Auntie Bev and Mum look so cheerified. I suppose I'll slither back upstairs and take this horrorvolting thing off.

Before I can slide away, Auntie Bev says, 'Ah, Time's wingéd arrow rushes on . . . and I must fly

2 blown kiss

. . . I shall love you and leave you.' She wraps her bedcover round herself and kisses her hand. She blows the kisses off her hand and over to us. Mum pretends to catch one. Auntie Bev whooshes round towards the door. Then, just as she's about to leave, she turns back to us and she says, 'Oh, by the way, daaaarlings, did you know that there's a guinea pig in Petal's basket?'

10
Petal is My Hero!

YIPPEEEEEEEEEEEEEEEEE!

I run as fast as I can to Petal's basket. And there he is!! There's Goliath, all snugly and guinea pigly, lying next to Petal. He's peeking out from under the blanket! I scoop him up and give him a special little hug.

Petal gets up and looks up at Goliath in my arms. Petal's wagging his funny little tail like anything. 'Good boy!' I say and he looks very pleased with himself. When I look back into the basket I can see there are some of Petal's biscuits on the blanket. 'Mum!' I say as Mum comes panting up behind me. 'Do you think Petal has been giving Goliath his biscuits? Look, there's a little pile of them right where Goliath was hiding!'

Baz with jewels on his overalls

'Well, I never!' says Mum. 'D'you know? I think good old Petal has been looking after his new friend for you!'

Dad comes in wearing his painting overalls. His overalls have jewels sewn on to the front. My dad likes to feel like Elvis Presley even when he's working. 'Well, blessa my soul . . .' he says when he sees

75

Goliath. Then I give Goliath to Mum while Dad and I do a bit of our Elvis dance routine, just to celebrate. Petal barks and waggles his bottom. Mum dances with Goliath so he doesn't feel left out.

We stop when we're puffed and Dad says, 'You're a sight for sore eyes, I must say, young Fizzy Freckles, all silver and shiny.'

'It's my star outfit,' I say. I don't feel quite so happified now I remember that I've got this space baby suit on.

'You should take that off now, before it gets spoiled,' says Mum. 'But first,' she says, handing Goliath to me, 'you must put this little body back in his cage and REMEMBER TO LOCK THE DOOR this time, all right?'

'Yes, Mum,' I say and I take Goliath back to the porch. I explain to him that he's safer in his cage than being liberated. I can see that he understands. And when Petal comes to sit next to the cage to keep him company he looks quite happy.

When I've taken off my silly star costume I put on my glamouroony glitteryfied jeans and my favourite sparkly T-shirt. (These have been glamouroonyfied by yours truly, Fizzy Pink.) Then I sit on the floor in my bedroom. My dad's painted huge flowers all over my walls. I helped with some of them. They are all different colours. I really love the flowers – they make me feel happy. And, of course, now that I've FOUND Goliath (or rather, Petal has found him) I don't feel so grottybags about liberating him. I could still make him a glittery coat and maybe a top hat.

I write a letter to Pixie and when I've finished I decide to go and see Mrs Fossil.

I pass Petal on the way out. He doesn't

dearest darlingest Pixie   BAZEEN MONDAY

GUESS WHAT??

← Petal found GOLIATH ! This is V.G. ← news!! ← sew

am ← KNOT ← stone cold dead ← OAR in ← prison after all

← bøt did tell a BFF (cos the ← BFF fairy <u>MADE</u> me)

everyone ← winks th am going 2 <u>THE</u> of ←plant

Bev's show. OOOPS! ← bøt it doesn't really ← mat+ter cos

no one will c the show anyway HOPE . l♥ve U 4 ever and ever - Fizzy

P.S. Did U know - if U ← lick a red ← smartie U can use it like a lipstick??

want to come with me this afternoon, as he's still guarding Goliath, so I give him a big hug.

guarding Goliath

Mrs Fossil is in her hall. She's rearranged her stuffed weasels and when I come in she is trying to move her stuffed bear. The bear is ginormous and it looks as if Mrs Fossil is dancing with it.

'Shall I help you?' I shout.

'Grab hold of a paw,' she says. 'See if

you can steer him down this end . . .' I do what she says and we bump the bear down the hall.

'Let's prop him up here,' says Mrs Fossil, puffing. We're standing by the front door. We push and pull the bear up on to his hind paws. He wobbles a bit but Mrs Fossil looks pleased.

'Don't you think he might scare people, standing right by the front door?' I ask.

'Stare at people?' she asks. 'Well, he can't help that, he's got glass eyes you see.'

'No. Frighten them,' I say.

'Biting them?' she says. 'No, no, he's not going to bite anyone – look,

Mrs Fossil moving her stuffed bear

he's only got two teeth!' Then she seems to forget about the bear and she says, 'What about a chocolate biscuit?' I nod my head in case she can't hear me say 'yes'.

I follow Mrs Fossil into her sitting room. It's really hot in here. She's got three electric fires on full blast. I have to eat my chocolate biscuits dead fast to stop all the chocolate melting and dripping on my fabberoony T-shirt.

'So, young Frizzy,' says Mrs Fossil when I've finished my fourth biscuit, 'tell me all the gossip!' There's something so friendly and batty about Mrs Fossil that I feel I can tell her everything. So I do. I tell her all about pretending that I am The Star and not just any old star in Auntie Bev's show. Then I tell her about my boring costume. How it isn't sparkly and it makes me look like a space baby. Then I explain about the Big Fat Fib Fairy and how telling fibs isn't really my fault.

When I've finished, she looks all excited. Don't know why. Until she says, 'Well, I can tell you I wouldn't miss this show for anything!' Oh, no! That's exactly what I DIDN'T want her to say! Doesn't Mrs Fossil realize that it would be a VERY BAD idea for people to see me?

'Really?' I say.

'No!' she cackles. 'I've already got my ticket and now that you've told me that you, little Frizzy, have got a great big fat part as a sparkly fairy from outer space AND that you're going to be singing "Twinkly Tinkle Little Star", well, I can hardly wait!'

YUCKYVOLTING, GROTTY HORRORBAGS!

11
Secrets and Sickbeds

When I get home from school the next day I check on Goliath straight away. He's 'all bright-eyed and bushy-tailed' (as Dad would say). I clean out his cage and then I have to wash my hands in case they are pooeyfied. I look at myself in the mirror above the basin and try out my superstar smile. Wish I *was* going to be The Proper Star. Cammy and her gang teased me all day about the star thing but I just tried not to listen to them. I know Mrs Fossil is bonkers but she did get all excited about seeing me in the show. Perhaps I could do something starry after all?

I do a few of the Elvis moves Dad has taught me. Then I try out some verses of 'Hound Dog' to see how it sounds. It sounds fabbybrill! It might be because I'm in the bathroom. Everything sort of

'Hound Dog' with Elvis moves

echoes and my voice comes out SO loud. Then I try doing the singing with the moves. I can't see right down to my feet in the mirror but the bit that I can see looks fridgey cool! Suddenly it is all clear to me. Somehow I *have* to be The Star of Auntie Bev's show . . . and I think I know just how I could do it!

Of course there is ONE thing that I could do to make myself feel more starry . . . I could sparkly up that boring old space baby outfit!

I tiptoe into Mum's sewing room and pick up the slithery silver costume. I have a good look at it and then I have a good look in the Odds and Bods box. I need to make sure that Mum won't find out what I'm going to do. I'd better put the baby suit back and go and find her.

She's in the kitchen. 'Hello, Fizzy Pops,' she says. 'I'm making mince pies! I

mince pies with cherries on top

thought I would make a great big pile of them and then I can put some in a tin to keep for Christmas and give some to Mrs Fossil. And if you are a very good girl there might be just one or two for us to have straight away.' Goody!

'The thing is . . .' I say, 'that I want to make a big surprise for you and Dad for Christmas.' (This is a Fib but it's only a teeny-weeny one so I'm sure it doesn't really count.) 'So I was *wondering* if you would let me do something dead private in your sewing room . . . I'll have to shut the door so you don't see the surprise . . .'

'Oh, Fizzy!' says Mum. 'That's ever such a sweet idea! A surprise! How lovely! Of course you can use my room. Just mind you don't damage any of the costumes, there's a good girl.'

'Oh, no!' I say, because I definitely won't

be *damaging* any of them – just *changing* one. 'I'll be about an hour,' I say.

I jump up the stairs, two at a time, and shut myself into Mum's sewing room. Then I find all the best, glitteriest, sparklified, glamouroony bits and bobs in Mum's box and set to work.

I sew as many sequins as I can manage on to the arms and legs of my costume. Then I attach lots and lots of long bits of glittery ribbon round the middle of the body part so that they hang down, like a grass skirt but sparkly. Then I find some gold, diamond-studded lace, which I stitch all over the top of the body. It looks FANTABBYMAZING!! I've taken much longer than an hour. Suddenly I hear Mum tapping at the door.

'Are you all right in there, Fizzy Freckles?' she asks.

'Oh, y-yes!' I say. 'But don't come in! Not yet!'

'I must come in in a minute,' she says. 'I have to finish off your costume tonight or I'll never have everything ready in time.'

HELP! What am I going to do now? I'd forgotten that Mum had said she still had some little things to do to my costume. The Big Fat Fib Fairy whispers in my ear . . .

'Don't worry, Mum,' I say. 'I've finished it for you!'

'Oooh, do let me see!' she says, and SHE STARTS OPENING THE DOOR!

'NOOOOO!' I yell. 'You mustn't come in – I haven't hidden your surprise and I've put my costume somewhere safe where the Splat won't splatter it – honestly, don't worry, it's all FABBY DOODLE . . .'

'Oh! Oh, well, as long as you promise that your outfit is safe . . .?' Mum sounds doubtful, but at least she's closing the door again. 'I will need to check it before the show,' she says.

'Honestly, Mum,' I say, 'it's right as nine pence.' (As Dad would say.) 'Don't worry!'

PHEW! That was a bit close! I quickly, quickly pull on the space baby suit to see how it looks.

WOW! It's turned into the most glamouroony disco outfit in the whole wide world! I make some of my moves in front of the long mirror. I look like the starriest superstar ever! I hold a piece of Mum's sequin ribbon round my head to finish the outfit off then I hear Mum at the door again!

'Fizzy? I really must come in now! I'll get in all of a tizzy if I can't get on with those costumes . . . I'm going to open the door in two seconds.'

Ooops-a-bloomin'-daisy! I haven't got

time to take my super duper disco glam rock outfit off in two seconds! I'll have to put my school uniform on over the top . . .

'There now,' says Mum as she pushes the door open. 'All done?'

'Um, yup,' I say. I can't say anything else on account of being all out of breath from dressing so fast.

'My word!' says Mum. 'You're getting a little bit roly-poly, Fizzy Freckles! Can't have you coming over all plumpish like me – I better watch you! No more fifth helpings of French toast for you, my girl! Now, help me pick all these bits and pieces up and then I can get on with Auntie Bev's costumes.'

There are a lot of bits and pieces all over the floor and by the time I have helped Mum pick them all up I am BOILED on account of all the clothes I'm wearing.

Mum looks at me. Then she comes up

and puts her hand on my forehead. 'Oh, deary me,' she says. 'I think you must be coming down with a fever! You're as hot as a hot buttered crumpet! Are you feeling poorly, my little duck?'

Now I, Fizzy Pink, am not stupid. If I can see a Really Good Opportunity skipping along towards me then I am definitely going to catch hold of its ankle and make it stop.

groaning

'OOOOOh!' I groan. 'I think I might be going to be sick . . . or maybe I'm going to faint . . . oooooh!'

'Right,' says Mum. 'There'll be no school for you tomorrow, Fizzy Freckles! There's only one place you should be and THAT is in bed!'

12
Tickle Test

Once you have caught hold of a Really Good Opportunity, it's a pity to let it go too soon. Specially when:

1) You're all tucked up cosy comfy in bed (except when you have to creep downstairs and make sure that Goliath is still safely in his cage).

2) Your mum brings you trays full of yumscrumptious things to eat.

3) YOU GET TO MISS SCHOOL. (Which means you miss maths. Sob – not!)

4) You have bags of time to listen to pop songs on the radio and sing along with them when you are sure that your mum can't hear.

merry Christmas from Fizzy

5) You get to be able to make all your Christmas cards and your mum doesn't get cross when you get glitter down the bed and glue on the sheets.

6) YOU GET TO MISS SCHOOL AGAIN THE NEXT DAY. (Because your mum wants to be sure that you are quite all right and 'one more day in bed won't hurt' – HEE HEE.)

93

7) You can try on your new glamouroony disco outfit and practise being The Star when your mum goes shopping AND

8) You can read Pixie's letter properly without being in a hurry to be on time for school.

Pixie thinks that I am a nutty nutcase for telling everyone that I am The Star of Auntie Bev's show. This makes me even more determined that I will *have* to make the Big Fat Fib come true. I WILL be The Star of the show – my public expects it of me, especially Mrs Fossil. I'll write back and let grumpy old Pixie know.

By the afternoon of my second day in bed I tell Mum that I'm feeling better. This is on account of beginning to feel bloomin' bored. It's all right being in bed when you

[eye] **Know** it wasn't very clever 2 say [eye] was THE [star] [boobs]+bøt U don't have 2 [bee] [snake] ←sew [bees] POOEY 2bout it. Anyway [eye] am in [bed] cos [bum]←tum thinks [eye] am [swirl] sick, he he [boobs]+bøt [eye]'m [eye]→ really. [eye] [fish] U were here dearest darlingest Pixie. If U were [eye] [log] WC show U my glamouroony [disc]←disc+o outfit [hand] we [log] WC put [bees]...er [tin]←tin our [face]←hair [hand] then We [log] WC do red smartie lipstick. It is [snoring] [flower]ing here without U. ♡U loads even if x U were [bees] Poo 2 me — ♡ Fizzy x x x

are ill but when you are pretending it gets a bit dullified after a while.

'I'm so pleased, Fizzy,' says Mum, 'especially because Auntie Bev wants you to go and rehearse your bit in the show this evening. Now let me have a proper look at you.'

I decide that going to a rehearsal would be less dullified than lying in bed. While I'm there I will be able to work out how I will be The Star. I make myself look all healthy while Mum has a look at me. I

loads of tea

can do this by smiling a lot and giggling when she tries her Tickle Test. Mum's Tickle Test is what she uses to see if I really am ill. If I don't giggle when she tickles me she knows it's serious.

'Wonderful!' says Mum. 'Up you get now and I'll give you your tea before we go to the rehearsal.'

Mum thinks I look way thinner when I get downstairs. I know that this is because I'm not wearing my fabberoony disco outfit under my clothes. Mum doesn't know this so she gives me loads of tea. This is yummy but it makes me feel a bit bad. I check to make sure that Goliath is OK. He is, which is also good. I feed him and then we go off to the village hall.

There are zillions of people in the village hall. Auntie Bev is shouting at them and telling them what they are supposed to be doing. It's all very muddly.

Suddenly all the lights in the hall go off and just the stage is lit up. A really old person creaks up and says a poem. This is dull. Auntie Bev sighs. The poem person walks off the stage. Someone a bit younger, but not much, comes on and does a tap dance. She has grey hair done up in a bun and really skinny legs. She's not very good but tap dancing looks like it might be fun. I know that I could do it miles better than her. I have a go in the corner of the hall and Auntie Bev tells me to 'Shhhh!'

At the end the tap dancing lady does a curtsy and topples over. Auntie Bev gets dead cross and shouts, 'Cynthia, if you can't stay upright, forget the curtsy please!' Cynthia looks as if she is about to say something back but Auntie Bev is not looking because she is beckoning me to go up on to the stage with her. She says, 'Now, everyone, could I have complete quiet while I do my act?' She whispers something to me about this being a 'marvellous piece of Shaky Pear' or something like that. Then she makes me stand at the back of the stage with my arms and legs out straight.

It's dead boring this Shaky Pear thing. Auntie Bev floats around the stage blahing on about fairies and her bottom. I think the fairies sound quite interesting but they don't come on, which is sobbysad.

I have to stand being a twinkly star for HOURS and HOURS. My arms get all achy and when I have to itch an itch on the end of my nose Auntie Bev starts squawking at me to stand still. This is NOT fun. I come to the conclusion that there is no way that I am going to waste all my starry talents standing still at the back of the stage while Auntie Bev drones on in front of me. After all, I've got my starry outfit, haven't I? And I've got my Elvis act. Besides, if there are any people coming to the show who are expecting me to be The Star I will jolly well HAVE to do my Elvis thing,

tap dancing lady

otherwise they will all know that I've fibbed, won't they?

13
An 'Actaw's' Life for Me!

The bad thing about passing Mum's Tickle Test and being well enough to be a star is that next morning I have to go back to school. It is Friday though. And early this morning Daisy phoned and asked if I was better. She said she'd missed me. I think that's dead nice.

Mum's a bit grumpy this morning. I know why – it's because she's got to finish all the costumes by Saturday lunchtime and that's tomorrow. At least she doesn't need to worry about my costume. I think she believed me when I told her that it was all done and that I had put it somewhere safe. Actually I've folded it up all neat and nice and hidden it in my pink rabbit pyjama case under all my knickers which are under my socks which have got a pile of T-shirts on top of them . . . so I hope she won't find it. Also I have made my bed, sort of, so Mum won't even need to go into my room. I hope.

I have to go straight to the classroom on account of being a bit late again.

When I get there Mrs SCary says,

rabbit pyjama case

'How nice of you to join us, FELICITY,' and you can tell she doesn't mean it AT ALL. Daisy gives me a big smile and that makes me feel better. I manage to pass her a note that I wrote at breakfast with my rainbow pen. It says

thankyou for ringing me.
Love from
    Fizzy
  X X X X X X X

and then I put all different-coloured kisses along the bottom. I don't think Pixie would mind about the kisses. I didn't put any hearts – I only put hearts for Pixie.

I'm thinking about how much Pixie

would like Goliath when I realize that Mrs SCary wants me to do something. At least I suppose it's me because she's shouting 'FELICITY!' and even though that's NOT my name, it usually means me.

'Yes, Mrs SCary?' I say.

'Perhaps you would be good enough to read out the next paragraph? We're on page twenty-two.' She says this bit with a growl in her voice.

reading like Aunty Bev

'Yes, Mrs SCary,' I say again, all polite. I open my book and try to find page twenty-two. When I've found it I decide to pretend to be Auntie Bev and read the paragraph out just like she would to get in some practice being The Star. I stand up and toss my hair around a bit. Then I clear my throat and hold the book up just below my face. I look straight ahead for a moment. This is what Auntie Bev calls 'focusing'. . .

'When you are QUITE ready!' says Mrs SCary.

And I begin.

It's hard work being Auntie Bev. I have to throw my arm about in a dramatic way that makes holding the book with the other hand very difficult. Also I have to speak in a posh 'actaw's' voice. This takes a lot of breath and, by the end of the paragraph, I'm puffed out. When I have finished reading I stay standing up while I close the book with a 'dramatic flourish', which is what Auntie Bev told someone to do last night at rehearsal. Then I sit down and wait for the applause . . .

There isn't any! Not a sausage!

Instead Mrs SCary glares at me and then she carries on with the lesson as if nothing has happened! Didn't she notice that I was being a brilliant 'actaw'? Obviously I am going to be at least a SQUILLION times more dramatic in Auntie Bev's show because there just might be someone there who will be expecting me to be The Star.

Cammy Sniggering

It's not very nice of Mrs SCary to ignore me. It's even not nicer when I turn round and see Cammy sniggering into the sleeve of her jumper. She whispers, 'Did you hear the *star*? Wasn't she *wonderful*? NOT!' All the other girls round her are sniggering too. Why doesn't Mrs SCary tell them to stop? But when I turn back Daisy gives me one of her dimply grins and she mouths 'Well done!' to me. This is nice of her – maybe I should tell Daisy the truth.

At break Cammy and her gang come up to me and Cammy says, 'So, what was the matter with you then? Did you have *star* flu? Ha Ha. Is the stress of being such a huge megastar too much for little you? Ha Ha. Is that why you weren't in school for two days?' I just scowl at them. 'What's the matter now?' Cammy says.

'Lost your voice after that brilliant piece of reading – not?'

The other girls all giggle.

'No,' I say.

'That's good because we wouldn't want the *star* to lose her voice before the Big Show, would we?' Cammy goes on. What does she mean by that? It almost sounds as if *she* might be coming to see Auntie Bev's show. But she wouldn't, would she?

'Oooh, no!' says Cammy's 'friend' Chrissy. 'It would be SO sad if Fizzy couldn't be the *star* of the show – we might all cry,' and then she pretends to sob and the others all start doing it too.

Well! How mean is that? But I DON'T CARE. I, Fizzy Pink, am worth twenty of any of them any old day . . . just because Cammy's jealous because she's not an 'actaw' like me, she thinks she's got to be mean to me. Well, YA BOO SUCKS, none of them is anywhere near being The Star in a Christmas show, are they? None of them believe that I could really do it. And they're just making it up, pretending that they might come to the show . . . I think it's a pity now that I won't have a chance to show them how starry I can be. I mean, none of them will really come, will they? Because I know that absolutely no one is interested in Auntie Bev's potty old show.

14

Star Light, Star Bright, I Wish I May, I Wish I Might . . .

'Oh, Fizzy!' says Mum. 'I'm so pleased to have finished all those costumes, I can tell you!'

It's Saturday afternoon and we are back in the village hall. There are loads of people and they are all buzzing about being busy. Mum and I have brought all the costumes with us and people are trying them on all over the place. I've got my super duper fabberoony disco-style star suit in my Barbie suitcase. I told Mum that I would look after it myself and as she's got piles of other things to do she didn't ask to see it, so that's OK.

Everyone is sort of giggly and excited. My tummy is jumping up and down a lot. There's hours to go before the show. Don't know why all these old people don't sit down and have a nap so as to be 'fresh as the morning dew' (as Dad would say).

Aunty Bev being a fairy queen

111

Instead the old poem person is fussing on about the spotlights. And the grey bun tap-dancing lady is practising her curtsy wearing the costume that Mum has made.

'Daaaarlings!' says Auntie Bev. 'The show must go on!' She looks happier today. 'Reenie, you are an angel! The costumes are DIVINE!' She's got her costume on. She says she's a fairy queen. She does look nice on account of my mum having made her a beautiful pale green fairy queen dress. It's got little wings. Wonder if she'll let me have the wings when she's finished?

Auntie Bev gives me lots of borifying jobs to do like sweeping the stage and washing up teacups. These are not the sorts of things that The Star should be doing. When I've done all the things she's asked me to do I go and sit in a corner and watch everything. All the people in the show are getting more and more grumpified. Someone has a big tantrum and Auntie Bev has to try to calm him down. She's not very good at calming people down because she's not very calm herself.

It's half an hour before 'curtain up'. All the people in the show are dead nervous. All except me, that is, because Stars NEVER get nervous. I am fridgey cool. Although I think I might have to whizz to the loo again – I've already been ten times so far! I've got on my glamouroony disco outfit and I've put my coat over the top. No one will know, until I go on stage, how glitteryfied I am. I decide that I'd better keep out of everyone's way so as not to make them even grumpier. I stand by the wings of the stage. These

are the curtains at the side and if I creep between two of them no one can see me. I imagine myself leaping on to the stage. I can hear the applause in my mind. I imagine all the huge bunches of flowers that my adoring fans will give me when I take my bow . . .

Suddenly I peek out from between the curtains and begin to look at the people coming in to watch the show. Bumpits crumpets! There are an awful lot of them! Why do all these people want to come and see Auntie Bev's boring old show? This is quite scarifying! I mean, LOOK at all these people! Look over there, there's Mrs Fossil and there is even someone who looks a bit like Daisy . . . IT IS DAISY . . . AAAAARGH! . . . She's come with her mum and dad!! She never said she was going to come! I will HAVE to be The Star of the show! She will never speak to me again when she finds out that I told a Big Fat Fib! And who's that behind her? OH, N-N-N-NOOOOOOOO! IT'S CAMMY!!!

CAMMY has come with two other snotty girls from school and their parents have come as well. They all think I am The Star! But I'm not really and it's not my fault, it was the Big Fat Fib Fairy – she made me do it and what am I going to do now? I could be sick . . . I might be sick . . . my tummy's gone all collywobbly and even though I am the bravest person in the entire universe my knees have started to shake . . . the curtain's going up . . . the show is starting . . .

'It's all right!' I tell myself, as the first act begins. 'Fizzy Pink does not get wibbly-wobbly.' I take lots of big breaths.

'No,' I say to myself as the second act starts, 'Fizzy Pink was Born To Be A Star and now she's going to be one . . . her audience expects it of her . . . (because she's told them a Big Fat Fib) . . . and now . . .' I go on, under my breath, 'now is your BIG MOMENT . . .'

starryfied outfit

It's time for Auntie Bev's bit. Auntie Bev is on the stage . . . I creep on behind her and hope she doesn't notice my overcoat. She does but she doesn't have time to do anything more than squeak to me to 'Take your coat OFF!' before the curtain goes UP. I can hear people tittering . . . This is not a good start.

Auntie Bev launches off into her borifying speech and I can see all these faces staring up at the stage. There are MILLIONS of them and I know that somewhere in there are Daisy and Cammy. I know what I have to do. I take one more look at all these people and I think, YES! I CAN DO THIS. I AM THE STAR!

I throw off my coat. Auntie Bev swings round with an amazed look on her face. I do a quick spin so that the ribbon skirt on my fabberoony disco outfit swings out like a fan. Then I start singing.

'You ain't nothin' but a hound dog . . .' I sing my loudest and make all the moves Dad has taught me. The audience looks dead surprised and Auntie Bev's mouth is flapping like a door in a gale. I'm really getting into it now. I'm wiggling and jiggling like anything. And then, suddenly, I've come to the end of the song! Now there should be stupendous applause, if they loved me. Oooooh, I hope they did!

What happens next is that there isn't stupendous applause because my dad stamps on from the wings and before anyone can begin to clap and cheer he picks me up and CARRIES ME OFF THE STAGE!

Then everyone laughs – a lot.

big blushifying moment

15

If I Could Find a Big Hole I Would Definitely Climb into It

'And just WHAT did you think you were doing, young lady?' Dad is scowling at me. He's scary when he's scowling. His eyebrows get all knotted together. We're home after the show and no one has said one single little word to me until now.

Mum and Dad are both standing in front of me in the kitchen with their hands on their hips.

'I'm sorry,' I say – because I am, truthfully.

'Well, I don't know, I must say,' says Mum. 'Poor Bev, you ruined her scene. You will have to apologize to her. I think we should go round and see her straight away.'

The ing

mum and Dad looking grumpyfied

We go round and apologize to Auntie Bev, which is Scary Mary had a Canary on account of Auntie Bev being mega angrified. Don't think she's going to give me her fairy wings after all.

When we've seen her, Mum says to me, 'Whatever made you do such a thing, Fizzy?'

Then I have to tell them EVERYTHING. All about the Big Fat Fib and about how then I HAD to be The Star.

Mum and Dad look dead angry. 'You know that we have told you never, ever to tell fibs, Fizzy,' says my mum, 'and look at the trouble you get yourself into when you do!'

'I'm sorry,' I say again because I can't think of anything else to say. They go on at me for a while about the Fib and then Mum says, 'I liked your outfit though!'

Dad starts chuckling and says, 'Mind you don't stick your elbows out when you do that spin in the middle of "Hound Dog" – you don't want to look like a chicken now, do you?'

On Monday morning at school Daisy is the first person I see. She says, 'My mum and dad and I thought you were

BAZEEN SUNDAY

dearest darlingest Pixie U were ← RIGHT

(eye) am a ← nutty ← nutcase.

tried 2 ThE ☆ of the show cos LOADS of people from school came to ← watch !!! M(eye) sort of friend ← daisy was there and ← cammy

← sew (eye) HAD 2 do something ☆y.

LA LA LA ← sang ← hounddog. (eye)

thought it was ·BRILLIBAGS· (face) but Dad carried me off the stage. It

was **HORROR VOLTING**·

(face) but colour R your new ? ← shell

(eye) ← make U 2 ·sparkly· badge 2

go on them? Love U 4 Always —
       x ♡ Fizzy x ♡ x

P.S. sorry I am such 2 noddy nit wit.

BRILLYBAGS in the show, Fizzy! Will you teach me to do all the moves, just like you?'

Daisy is so fabberoony. Maybe next time (if there is a next time) I will tell Pixie AND Daisy the truth from the start. No one else at school is nice though. Cammy and her gang are horrorvolting to me. They start singing 'You're exactly like a hound dog . . .' under their breath whenever they see me. Then they all giggle and wiggle their bottoms a bit like I do when I'm making my moves. In lunch break I see them all pretending to be me. They can't do the moves well at all though. Even so, it makes me feel horrorvolting to see them.

During Sharing

a real hound dog wiggling his bottom

Time I don't say anything. Mrs SCary asks me if I'm feeling all right! She looks quite worried, as if she might care a teeny-weeny bit about me. I tell her that I am fine but that I am resting my vocal chords. This makes the others laugh again so I shut up.

It's not a very nice feeling having people laugh at you, even if you are Fizzy Pink, the Bravest Person in the World. If it wasn't for Daisy and the fact that it's not long until the Christmas holidays, I think I would like to zoom off into the night and become a real star. Then I could hang around in the sky zillions of miles away and no one could ever be grottybags to me ever again.

After lunch we have to write a story. Mrs SCary says that the title of the story has to be 'The Worst Day of My Life'. Lots of people in my class, most especially the boys, start groaning and saying things like 'I don't know what to write . . . can't I write about something else . . .?' But I know EXACTLY what I'm going to write about and I begin straight away.

I write loads and loads but I still finish ages before anyone else. I use my last piece of paper to write again to Pixie.

dearest darlingest Pixie 👁 am small ✿ cos 👁 am s'posed 2 ✿ story 🐮 bət 👁 have finished. My Story is called The WORST day of my LIFE. I 🐮 bət U know wot 👁 🦌 or goat about!! 👁 🐟 U could come and stay at 🌲 time.

story writing stinky school ↙ writing this ← writing a

Do U think your 🏠 ← tum 🪵 let U? It 🪵 ✿ FABBEROONY. Nothing at School is FABBEROONY — ✿ daisy is the only 1 who is 🙂 2 me 🐮 bət It's ⊶ the same as having U here ···· MRS SCARY is looking at me ···· better go ···· ♡U x Fizzy x ♡ x

16

SCary Smiles!

I am SO happified when the end of term is almost here. Mostly everyone has stopped being piggy about me starring in Auntie Bev's show but Cammy and her gang still pretend to do 'Hound Dog' moves when they see me.

When I brought Goliath back to school Mrs SCary looked dead surprised to see him looking so chubby and well. She said I had cared for him 'very nicely', which is the first good thing she has ever, EVER said to me. (Bet poor old Goliath won't look nearly as fabby after Cammy has looked after him.)

Since telling the Big Fat Fib about being The Star, the Big Fat Fib Fairy has often tried to make me tell other Big

the Splat eating paper chains

Fat Fibs in class but I haven't let her. I haven't told ANY fibs. Well, hardly any, anyway.

Dad has finished painting our house. He did his and Mum's bedroom last. It's pink with pale blue and white stripes. Mum says she feels just like a princess in it. She's made lacy curtains with crystal beads hanging off them. They look brillybags.

The Splat and Petal and I have made loads and loads of paper chains and glittery snowflakes. Well, Petal and the Splat didn't *really* make them. In fact, between them they ate most of the glitter and half the paper chains. But the house looks beautiful, all Christmasified. It's almost as nice as our old house except that Pixie doesn't live next door.

It's the very last day of term and Mum and Dad have to come into school this afternoon for an end of term thing-a-me-jig. It's when the head teacher borifies on about what's happened during the term. Then we all sing carols. We've been practising them for ages. I like carols. They sound best if you sing them really loud and that's something that I'm fabby dabby at.

After lunch we have to wait for our parents to arrive. When they do arrive we have to show them to their seats and be all polite even though they are only our parents.

Mum and Dad come quite early. I don't mind now if people see them in Dad's pink van with 'Any Colour As Long As It's Pink' written along the side. I think it's quite fridgey cool. Loads of the boys (who don't really count) have said they think 'It's wicked' and they would like to have a ride in it.

My mum is wearing a dress and a jacket that she has made herself. They are 'pillar-box red' according to Mum. She has

at the school thing-a-me-jig

put white fluffy fur all round the collar of the jacket and round the bottom of the dress. She looks a bit like Mother Christmas. She's made the Splat a little green suit as well. He looks like an elf. Dad has got his Elvis leather jacket on and his sparkly Elvis boots. They look so glamouroony, I feel dead proud of them. I wish I could make them proud of me.

'Fizzy!' says my mum, all excited, when she sees me. 'You'll *never* guess what!'

'What?' I ask.

'I spoke to Pixie's mum this morning and she says that Pixie can come and stay straight after Christmas! What do you think of that?'

'What I think of that,' I say as I give Mum a great big hug, 'is that this is the BEST news ever! I can't wait for Christmas,' I say.

'I thought you might like to ask little

Daisy over while Pixie is with us. Would you like to do that?' asks Mum.

'Oh!' I say. 'Don't know.' I've got to think a lot about this. It would be lovely, if Pixie didn't mind. I'm sure she would like Daisy . . .

But now I've got to show Mum and Dad to their seats because I can see Mrs SCary and she's looking at me. I think she might be ill. She's making a very peculiar face. Wait a minute! I think she might be SMILING! She must be looking at someone else. I spin round to see who is standing behind me but there isn't anyone. When I look back Mrs SCary isn't looking at me any more so I think I must have imagined the smile.

'It's going to be deadly borifying,' I say when Mum and Dad are sitting down. 'Hope you don't mind.'

'A little less conversation . . .' Dad

croons. 'It's time you went and sat down, young Fizzy Freckles – don't you worry about us. We're doing just fine.'

The thing-a-me-jig goes on for ages. The Head drones on for hours and hours. My bottom is getting achy and my eyes keep on wanting to be shut. Suddenly I see Mrs SCary get up. I think, Uh-oh! What am I going to get squawked at for this time? But she doesn't squawk at all. What she does is to say, 'I have a prize to give out now!' This sounds more interesting. She goes on, 'Although the Head and I will never approve of telling any sort of untruths, sometimes, when the person who has told an untruth has learned their lesson, something very special happens. This is what has occurred in this case. Because of an untruth, a member of my class produced an exceptional piece of work. I would therefore like to give this term's prize for the Best Story, entitled "The Worst Day of My Life", to – FELICITY Pink!'

THAT'S ME!

Everyone is clapping and Mrs SCary beckons me up on to the stage. Well, I can tell you, I don't need to be asked twice. I'm up on that stage quicker than you can say superstar!

When the clapping has stopped, Mrs SCary says, 'Before I give FELICITY her prize' – I am trying REALLY hard not to tell everyone that my name is Fizzy – 'perhaps you would all like to hear her story?'

Loads of people say, 'Yes, please,' so Mrs SCary hands me my story and then she goes and sits down.

So here I am! Standing in front of all these people and they are all looking at me and waiting for me to begin. I feel fabberoony! I look at everyone and smile my most glamouroony smile. I like it up here. I push back my hair and hold my story up just under my face. I 'focus' just like a real 'actaw' and then I begin.

I get to the bit where I do my 'Hound Dog' performance at Auntie Bev's Christmas show. I suddenly see one of those Good Opportunities bouncing along towards me. I grab hold of it. I put down my story and launch myself into my own version of 'Hound Dog' with all the moves (but I keep my elbows in this time).

There's such a cheer when I've finished that I have to do it all again! At the end I look at the audience and EVERYONE is grinning and clapping and cheering, especially Mum and Dad and the Splat. Mum and Dad are looking dead proud.

Then I see Cammy. She's not smiling.

She's looking
deadly
daggers
at the
rest of
her gang
who are
laughing and
cheering.
When she
catches me
looking at her

the Star!

she makes the most disgusterous face at me, but I don't care because I know that she's just plain old jealous of my fabberoony 'Hound Dog'.

This is the best, bestest day of my life so far. And guess what? When Mrs SCary gives me my prize I see that it's a fantasibrill, glamouroony, great, big, shiny, silver STAR!

♡ ♡ ♡

dearest darlingest Pixie

U R coming to ~~xxx~~ ← st hay

with ME!!!! [eye] am [drawing] sew

[smiley] t[hat]hat [eye] can't (STOP) [boat]!

[hand] guess wot??? [eye] 1 2

-PRIZE- 4 my

Story!!! My prize is a [star]

it is soooooo glamouroony!!!

[log] U like to [meat] ← meat my new

friend [flower] ← daisy at [tree] ???

[eye] [face] think U [log] like

her. [eye] [N] ←h rope [Santa] ← father christmas

gives me some glitter pens — wot

do U want??? Can't WAIT 2

C U!! All my♡ 4 ever and ever

and ever — FIZZY ♡ ♡

x ♡ x ♡ x

things to make:
☆ STARS ☆

← Cut out a felt star (white could be a good colour to choose)

← Put your star on a piece of paper and spread a thin layer of PVA glue over it.

Sprinkle on gold or silver glitter and LEAVE TO DRY (boring!) →

← Stitch or stick on some sequins or beads - or both if you're feeling v. fabberoony

← carefully sew a safety pin on the back

← then you can make zillions more and pin them EVERYWHERE! GLAMOUROONY!

you could do cleverclogs blanket stitching around the edge which would be fantasibrill!!

how to make Elvis moves:

tie spoon to stand of Mum's dress-making dummy for microphone →